Hello, Family Members,

Learning to read is one of the most importan of early childhood. **Hello Reader!** books are children become skilled readers who like to read. Beginning readers learn to read by remembering frequently used words like "the," "is," and "and"; by using phonics skills to decode new words; and by interpreting picture and text clues. These books provide both the stories children enjoy and the structure they need to read fluently and independently. Here are suggestions for helping your child *before*, *during*, and *after* reading:

Before

- Look at the cover and pictures and have your child predict what the story is about.
- Read the story to your child.
- Encourage your child to chime in with familiar words and phrases.
- Echo read with your child by reading a line first and having your child read it after you do.

During

- Have your child think about a word he or she does not recognize right away. Provide hints such as "Let's see if we know the sounds" and "Have we read other words like this one?"
- Encourage your child to use phonics skills to sound out new words.
- Provide the word for your child when more assistance is needed so that he or she does not struggle and the experience of reading with you is a positive one.
- Encourage your child to have fun by reading with a lot of expression . . . like an actor!

After

- Have your child keep lists of interesting and favorite words.
- Encourage your child to read the books over and over again. Have him or her read to brothers, sisters, grandparents, and even teddy bears. Repeated readings develop confidence in young readers.
- Talk about the stories. Ask and answer questions. Share ideas about the funniest and most interesting characters and events in the stories.

I do hope that you and your child enjoy this book.

—Francie Alexander
Reading Specialist,
Scholastic's Learning Ventures

To Jane
— G.M.

To the child in all of us.
— R.C.

Text copyright © 2001 by Grace Maccarone.
Illustrations copyright © 2001 by Richard Courtney.
All rights reserved. Published by Scholastic Inc.
SCHOLASTIC, HELLO READER, CARTWHEEL BOOKS and associated logos are trademarks and/or registered trademarks of Scholastic Inc.

Library of Congress Cataloging-in-Publication Data

Maccarone, Grace.
Dinosaurs / by Grace Maccarone ; illustrated by Richard Courtney.
p. cm. — (Hello reader! Level 2)
Summary: Simple text and illustrations present different kinds of dinosaurs.
ISBN 0-439-20060-1
1. Dinosaurs — Juvenile literature. [1. Dinosaurs.] I. Courtney, Richard ill. II. Title. III. Series.

QE861.5 .M33 2001
567.9 — dc21
00-025984

10 9 8   02 03 04 05

Printed in the U.S.A.   24
First printing, February 2001

DINOSAURS

by Grace Maccarone
Illustrated by Richard Courtney

Hello Reader! Science — Level 2

Cartwheel
·B·O·O·K·S·®

SCHOLASTIC INC.
New York Toronto London Auckland Sydney
Mexico City New Delhi Hong Kong

Dinosaurs lived
long ago.

Fossils tell us
what we know.

Some were big.

Some were small.

Some were long.

Some were tall.

Some had beaks.

Some had sails.

Some had plates
and powerful tails.

Some had spikes

or bird-like feet.

Some ate plants.

And some ate meat.

Some had horns and bony frills.

Some had fancy crests and bills.

Some had sharp claws.

Some had strong jaws.

Some dinosaurs
fought each other.

Some of the young stayed
close to mother.

Some dinosaur eggs
hatched in a nest.

Which dinosaur do you like best?

Diplodocus

Ultrasaurus

Saltopus

Tyrannosaurus

Spinosaurus

Struthiomimus

Ankylosaurus

Stegosaurus

Iguanodon

Hypsilophodon

Dryosaurus   Allosaurus

Triceratops

Apatosaurus

Deinonychus

Lambeosaurus

Protoceratops

Velociraptor

Homalocephale

Ceratosaurus

Maiasaura